For Will, Brad, and Erin, who have journeyed with me.
—D. D.

For anyone who has ever lost someone.
—A. L.

Text copyright © 2019 Danielle Davison. Illustrations copyright © 2019 Anne Lambelet. First published in 2019 by Page Street Kids, an imprint of Page Street Publishing Co., 27 Congress Street, Suite 105 Salem, MA  01970. www.pagestreetpublishing.com All rights reserved. No part of this book may be reproduced or used, in any form or by any means, electronic or mechanical, without prior permission in writing from the publisher. Distributed by Macmillan, sales in Canada by The Canadian Manda Group. ISBN-13: 978-1-62414-765-4.  ISBN-10: 1-62414-765-8. CIP data for this book is available from the Library of Congress. This book was typeset in Minion Pro. The illustrations were done digitally. Printed and bound in Shenzhen, Guangdong, China. Page Street Publishing uses only materials from suppliers who are committed to responsible and sustainable forest manage-ment. Page Stree Publishing protects our planet by donating to nonprofits like The Trustees, which focuses on local land conservation.
19 20 21 22 23 CCO 5 4 3 2 1

# The Traveler's Gift

## A Story of Loss and Hope by Danielle Davison

### illustrated by Anne Lambelet

PAGE STREET KIDS

Liam's father was a sailor. After returning from sea, he'd weave tales for Liam of the faraway places he'd been and the curious things he'd seen, using just his words.

Someday, Liam would join his father. They would travel to faraway places, and Liam would have stories of his own to tell. But for now, he was happy retelling his father's stories to anyone who would listen.

But one day, his father didn't return.

Liam thought of the stories he hadn't heard, the ones he'd never hear again, and the adventures they would never take. All the magic he once felt retelling his father's stories faded.

Liam spent his days alone at the harbor. He watched
the ships pass by, and though he knew his father
wouldn't return, he searched for him among the
sea of people.

At night, Liam would listen to the old men tell their
tales of life at sea. But none of them could weave
stories with their words the way his father had.

One day, while Liam watched some men unload a barge, a very old man arrived at the harbor. His name was Enzo, but the other men called him "the Traveler."

The Traveler was unlike anyone Liam had ever seen. He seemed wise and had a long, colorful beard. When the Traveler spoke of his voyages, a peculiar thing happened: His beard grew. And grew. And grew, until each story he told wove from his face like a tapestry.

People journeyed from afar to catch a glimpse of the Traveler's magical beard.

"Would you look at that?" marveled one person.

"How odd," said another.

Only Liam didn't think the Traveler's beard was odd. He thought it perfect for a man whose words wove splendid pictures, the way his father's once had.

One day, the Traveler made an announcement. He was ready to take his final voyage to sea. "I am old and tired, and ready to pass on my gift," he said. "I need a worthy companion to travel with me to unknown lands. Upon returning, he must share his tales of adventure with the people he meets," he said.

Something stirred inside Liam.
*Maybe I could be a worthy companion.*
Although he doubted the Traveler would choose a quiet child like him, Liam raised his hand.

"Me?" whispered Liam.

"Yes, you," replied the Traveler.

They set sail. "I feel like my heart might burst from my chest!" said Liam.

The Traveler smiled. "I felt that way on my first voyage too."

As they traveled, Enzo taught Liam to listen,
really listen, to the world around him.

And he taught him how to see things,
truly see things, with more than just his eyes.

They traveled to places that could not be found on a map, and met people with souls as curious as their own.

They saw unforgettable places and encountered unusual creatures. And Liam was happy . . .

"I never want our journey to end," he whispered.
"Neither do I," said Enzo.

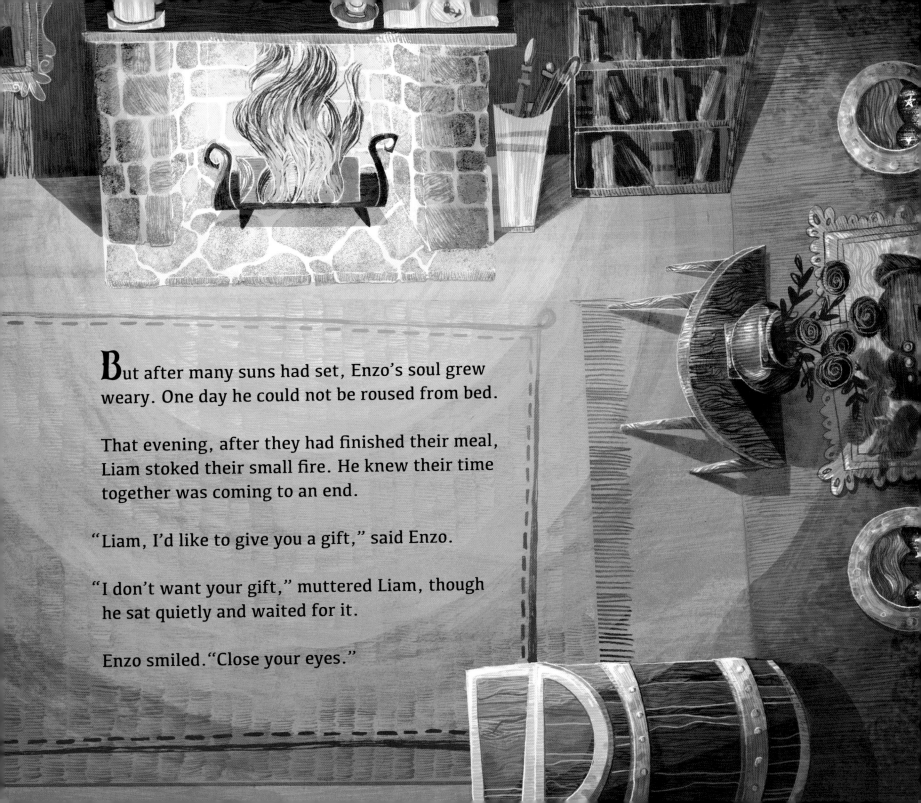

But after many suns had set, Enzo's soul grew weary. One day he could not be roused from bed.

That evening, after they had finished their meal, Liam stoked their small fire. He knew their time together was coming to an end.

"Liam, I'd like to give you a gift," said Enzo.

"I don't want your gift," muttered Liam, though he sat quietly and waited for it.

Enzo smiled. "Close your eyes."

Liam closed his eyes, but nothing happened.

"Tell me a story," said Enzo. Liam was confused.

"What story would you like me to tell?" Liam asked.

"That is up to you," answered Enzo.

They sat in silence as the embers of their fire flickered.
Finally, Liam spoke. "There is one story I'd like to tell."

As day faded into night and night into day, Liam told his story.

He spoke of the father he had lost, the friend he had found, and the adventures they had taken together. Liam's words wove splendid pictures, the way his father's once had.

Liam felt the magic of storytelling
he thought he'd lost.

And as Liam's words wove the tale of
his and the Traveler's final adventure,
the Traveler gave Liam his gift.

And it was wondrous.